Sebastian waits at the bus stop....

BUS STOP

He waits a very long time

Sebastian climbs on
board

The driver is....

A cow!!

Good Morning !

Says the cow

Sebastian goes to sit down

All the passengers are animals !

He sits next to
a hedgehog

OUCH!!!

I think I'll move...

But the snake is scary

and the bear is

So big...

He spots some stairs

I'll help you up

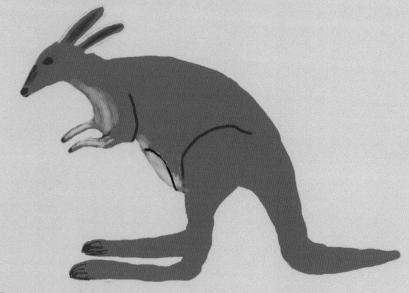

says the kangaroo.

Hop in my pouch

She hops up the stairs

And now Sebastian is on
the top deck

He sits right at the front

The cars look tiny

Watch out for that tree, he shouts

LOW BRIDGE

And the low bridge

The bus stops at a
lovely green meadow

Would you like to drive now? Asks the cow

Yes!   says Sebastian

But I can't reach the steering wheel

The friendly pig helps out

Now you've got a cushion!

Can we help too?

say the hare
and the tortoise

Yes! Take a foot pedal each

Hare jumps on the accelerator and the bus takes off

10pmh, then 20, 30, 50, 80....
100mph!!

Quick, tortoise.....Help!

Tortoise slowly slowly
steps on the brake

And the bus stops

Sebastian climbs out,
and runs home for tea

Printed in Great Britain
by Amazon